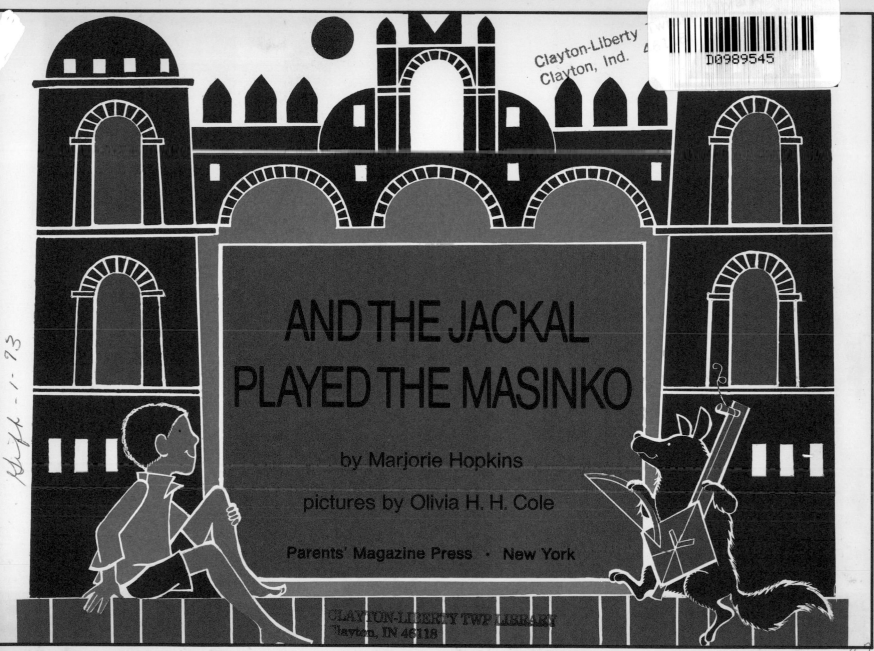

AND THE JACKAL PLAYED THE MASINKO

by Marjorie Hopkins

pictures by Olivia H. H. Cole

Parents' Magazine Press · New York

For those charming householders, Liz and Bernie O'Brien

Once there lived in Ethiopia a boy whose name was Haptu. He shared a simple tukal-hut with his Uncle Ras and their three animal servants.

Now the animals all had good in them. The jackal didn't run away, the warthog didn't steal salt from the ingot, and the monkey took only his share of the roasted chick-peas.

But none of them would obey Haptu.

Every morning Uncle Ras told Haptu, "Keep the servants at their jobs." Then he went out to sow millet or reap it in the hot sun.

Haptu sat down to learn his letters. Then—trouble!

Use the pestle and not your hoofs when you grind teff for the flat-bread," Haptu told the warthog.

The warthog sniffed. "My hoofs grind it faster."

"You've not swept behind the yellow chest," Haptu scolded the monkey, whose job it was to keep the tukal-hut clean.

The monkey laughed and shook his kosso-leaf broom almost in Haptu's worried face.

But the worst one was the jackal. It was his job to play restful music in the evenings.

"Please learn to play a new tune on your masinko!" Haptu begged.

"I know this one well. I won't learn another," the jackal yawned, sawing his bow lazily across the one string of the masinko.

Uncle Ras was always too tired when he came home at night to hear tales about the animals' naughty ways.

But one day the animals did no work at all. They sat around laughing and telling stories.

Haptu ran to Uncle Ras who was cutting down the thorny cantuffa plants around his fields.

Uncle Ras listened to Haptu's complaints. He said nothing, but suddenly he turned back to his work and began cutting down the cantuffa faster and faster.

Haptu watched, fearing his uncle was displeased with him.

Uncle Ras worked angrily until there was nothing left but stubble.

Just as he had finished, who should come riding along but the King of Ethiopia!

Haptu and Uncle Ras bowed low, though Haptu wanted to look at the King's brocade robe and rhinoceros-horn ornament.

The King stopped and his umbrella-holder waited behind him. "What a good man you are!" the King told Uncle Ras. "You have cleared the cruel cantuffa from your ruler's path. Tomorrow you may come to the palace at Debra Tabor and receive your reward."

That night Uncle Ras sent the animals to bed and talked alone with Haptu over their dish of wheat and bean porridge.

"I am old and ugly," said Uncle Ras. "You are young and eager for adventure. You go to court for me."

"What will the King give me?" Haptu asked excitedly.

"He may ask you what you want," said Uncle Ras. "Don't be greedy of course. I'll send the animals with you for protection from bandits."

Next morning Uncle Ras scrubbed Haptu and the three animals in the village pond and waved them off to Debra Tabor.

For a while they walked along peacefully.
Then, as they came within sight of Debra
Tabor's round, stone roofs, the animals
began to tease Haptu.

"*We* should have the reward," whined the
jackal. "We made Uncle Ras angry enough
to chop down all the cantuffa. For myself
I'd like a few gurramailie-bird feathers
to brighten me up on holidays."

"I've always wanted an embroidered
cotton shawl," said the warthog dreamily,
"a fine one."

"For me," said the monkey, "a fly-whisk!
What else adds so much dignity to the
bearer?"

So they went on, urging Haptu to promise to ask for these things.

When they stopped for lunch and Haptu was busy dividing the flat-bread, the jackal whispered to the monkey, "We'll refuse to go farther until he *has* promised."

Haptu heard the whisper. And after the animals had curled up for naps, he sat thinking for a little while. Then he rose and trotted on toward Debra Tabor alone.

He soon came to the city. The palace stood in a grove of wanzy trees, and white fountains sent cool sprays among the lower branches. A guard led Haptu inside where the King sat on a great throne. The King's little daughter sat on a cushion at his feet.

Your uncle has sent you?" the King asked graciously enough. "You may name your reward. What do you wish?"

"O, King," said Haptu, "on my way here I saw three animals asleep under a fence. I would like to have them to serve my uncle and me."

"Find these animals and bring them to the palace," the King told his men.

Soon the men returned, carrying the monkey, the warthog and the jackal in a rope net. They all looked very frightened, and Haptu could almost hear them thinking, *What has Haptu told the King about us?*

The King frowned.

"These are not very attractive animals," he said.

But they're very clever," said Haptu. "The warthog can grind teff with a pestle. The monkey can sweep and clean splendidly. And the jackal, I've heard, can learn to play a new tune on the masinko every week."

"Is this true?" the King asked the animals.

The animals all nodded hard.

"Take them home, then," said the King. "But first you must have, as well, a robe of brocade and slippers of brocade and a hood. My tailors will make them for you in the robing room."

The King's tailors worked quickly. In no time, Haptu stood stiff with brocade. The animals watched him from a corner, but Haptu did not once look at them.

The King's little daughter watched, too, her eyes soft and smiling. "You don't look very comfortable in your new clothes," she laughed.

"I'm not," Haptu admitted quickly. "I think if I just had a cotton shawl to tuck here between my shoulders where the seam scratches. . . . A few gurramailie-bird feathers in my slippers would keep the threads from pricking. And a fly-whisk would help very much, for the hood is so warm."

The King's little daughter laughed merrily again and sent the tailors to get the shawl and the feathers and the fly-whisk, one with a golden handle.

Then, as Haptu and the animals left the palace grounds, she waved good-bye from among the wanzy trees.

On the way home, the animals said very little. As soon as Debra Tabor was behind them, Haptu shed his brocade robe and gave it to the warthog to carry. Then he wrapped the embroidered shawl about the warthog's neck.

"Use the pestle! Use the pestle!" the warthog hissed softly to himself as he walked along balancing his load.

The jackal hummed new tunes, being careful not to shake loose the feathers that Haptu had tucked under his collar.

The monkey swept twigs and pebbles from the path with his golden-handled fly-whisk, to get in practice.

When they reached home again, Haptu made his brocade robe into a fat pillow for Uncle Ras.

That evening Uncle Ras said to Haptu, "How clean the tukal-hut looks. How smooth the teff is! How comfortable it is to lean against this beautiful pillow! And I like the new tune our jackal plays."

"Yes," Haptu said, winking at the jackal, "I think we'll all be more comfortable from now on."

And the jackal winked back from behind his masinko.